CASE #1
THE MAGIC BOX

the GHOST and MAX MONROE

CASE #1
THE MAGIC BOX

WRITTEN BY **L.M. FALCONE**

ILLUSTRATIONS BY **KIM SMITH**

KIDS CAN PRESS

To my great nieces, Nadya, Gabriella, Emma, Emily, Maya and Daniella
– I love you to bits! And to Terry Kennedy – my partner in crime.

Text © 2014 L. M. Falcone
Illustrations © 2014 Kids Can Press

Kids Can Press acknowledges the financial support of the Government of Ontario, through the Ontario Media Development Corporation's Ontario Book Initiative; the Ontario Arts Council; the Canada Council for the Arts; and the Government of Canada, through the CBF, for our publishing activity.

Published in Canada by
Kids Can Press Ltd.
25 Dockside Drive
Toronto, ON M5A 0B5

Published in the U.S. by
Kids Can Press Ltd.
2250 Military Road
Tonawanda, NY 14150

www.kidscanpress.com

Edited by Yasemin Uçar
Designed by Marie Bartholomew
Illustrations by Kim Smith
Chapter icon illustrations by Andrew Dupuis

The hardcover edition of this book is smyth sewn casebound.
The paperback edition of this book is limp sewn with a drawn-on cover.
Manufactured in Malaysia, in 3/2014, by Tien Wah Press (Pte.) Ltd.

CM 14 0 9 8 7 6 5 4 3 2 1
CM PA 14 0 9 8 7 6 5 4 3 2 1

Library and Archives Canada Cataloguing in Publication

Falcone, L. M. (Lucy M.), 1951–, author
    The ghost and Max Monroe. Case #1, The magic box /
written by L. M. Falcone ; illustrated by Kim Smith.

(The ghost and Max Monroe)
ISBN 978-1-77138-153-6 (bound)   ISBN 978-1-77138-017-1 (pbk.)

I. Smith, Kim, 1986–, illustrator II. Title. III. Title: Magic box.

PS8561.A574G46 2014   jC813'.6   C2013-908316-2

Kids Can Press is a **CØRUS**™ Entertainment company

CONTENTS

Chapter 1 7

Chapter 2 12

Chapter 3 18

Chapter 4 24

Chapter 5 29

Chapter 6 34

Chapter 7 38

Chapter 8 43

Chapter 9 51

Chapter 10 55

Chapter 11 59

Chapter 12 65

Chapter 13 70

Chapter 14 75

CHAPTER 1

HOW CHEAP ARE YOU? BAZAAR

Dark clouds moved along with Max Monroe
and his grandpa Harry as they drove down
the dirt road that led to Harry's house. Max
hadn't been there since he was a little kid.

Max's mom died two years ago, so he
lived with just his dad. His dad was a news
reporter for a major TV station. He covered
stories all over the world. Usually, Harry
came to look after Max when his father
was away. But lately, his father was gone
for longer and longer periods of time.

There was a family meeting, and it was decided that Max should move in with his grandpa for the summer. Today was the day.

"I forgot!" shouted Harry, slamming on the brakes.

"Forgot what, Grandpa?" asked Max, prying his fingers off the dashboard.

"The How Cheap Are You? Bazaar! It closes in five minutes! Hang on, Max!"

Harry spun the car around and drove like a maniac. In exactly four and a half minutes, they arrived at the bazaar. Harry leaped out of the car and pounded down the steps. Max ran after him. Inside, he spotted Harry standing in front of two large tables covered with mystery books. He and his grandfather *loved* reading mysteries.

THAT LOOKS LIKE A GARBAGE BAG TO ME

Fill a bag — only $5.00, said the sign. Harry pulled out a huge green bag. The lady standing next to him frowned. "Wait just a minute here. That looks like a *garbage* bag to me."

Harry grinned. "Madam, the sign says, *Fill a bag*. Well, *this* — is a bag!"

The lady scratched her head. Harry snapped open the bag. It was so big you could fit a moose in it. One hundred and sixty-four mysteries got jammed inside.

Harry and Max drove to Harry's house in the country. Max smiled when he saw it. It was the kind of house every kid loves — old and spooky looking, with black shutters and vines crawling around the windows.

As they pulled into the driveway, water drops began to plop on the windshield. Then the rain came down in buckets. It didn't stop for a week.

Forced to stay inside, Max and his grandfather ate tons of popcorn and read mystery books — dozens of them.

SOMEONE WAS CRYING

The sun finally came out on a Saturday morning. Max slipped into his jeans and T-shirt and went outside. Harry didn't believe in lawn mowers, so the grass was almost as tall as Max. He waded through it until he came to a tree. Grabbing the lowest branch, he began climbing. Higher and higher he went. Suddenly, he heard a sound …

Someone was crying.

The sound was coming from behind him. Max climbed back down and headed toward some bushes. He parted them and stepped through. Standing in front of him was a run-down house, smaller than Grandpa Harry's, with an old wooden sign that said *The Monroe Detective Agency*.

CHAPTER 2

THE OLD POOP NEVER SOLVED ONE MEASLY CASE

Max rushed into the kitchen and found Harry swinging on a hammock that was hanging in the big bay window.

"Grandpa, you never told me you were a *detective*."

Harry shoveled a spoonful of cereal into his mouth. "You never asked."

"I'm asking now."

"Fair enough. I was never a detective, Max."

Harry reached over and lifted a can of whipped cream off the table, then settled back in the hammock.

"How do you explain the sign?"

"What sign?"

"The Monroe *Detective* Agency sign."

"Oh, *that* sign," said Harry. "My brother, Larry, was a detective." Max looked impressed. But Harry shook his head. "He wasn't very good," he went on. "The old poop never solved *one* measly case."

"Really?"

"Really." Harry shot whipped cream over his cornflakes. "The whole town laughed at him. Newspapers wrote about him. They called him the 'bumbling detective.' It broke his heart. That's how he died — of a broken heart."

"Why did no one ever tell me you had a brother who died?"

"He never left, so I don't think of him as dead."

Max's eyes widened.

"Well, he's *dead*," said Grandpa Harry, "but his ghost still haunts the detective agency."

CRYING GHOSTS ... HAUNTED DETECTIVE AGENCIES

Max pulled up a chair and sat beside his grandfather. "Your brother, Larry, is a *ghost?*"

"Yup."

"And he *haunts* the detective agency in the backyard?"

"Yup." Harry shot some whipped cream into his mouth, then set the can back on the table. "Sometimes he hangs around the house. But mostly, he sits in the coach house, bawling his eyes out."

"I heard crying!"

"That'd be Larry. He likes to have a good cry around this time of day."

Max shook his head. "Crying ghosts … haunted detective agencies." He was talking to himself now. "I'll wake up any minute and everything will be normal."

"Hi-dee-ho!" said a voice.

Max spun around.

MAYBE YOU SHOULD SIT DOWN

Harry smiled. "Max, meet your great-uncle Larry."

The color drained from Max's face.

"You don't look well," said the voice.

"Maybe you should sit down."

"I am sitting down."

"See what I mean?" Harry laughed. "Dumb as a doorknob."

"Harry tells me you're hooked on detective stories," said the voice. "Come on. I'll show you my office."

Max didn't move.

"Why don't you let Max see you first, Larry?" suggested Harry.

"Sure. No problem."

A man appeared, right out of thin air. He had a friendly face and bushy hair that stuck out all over, and there was no color to him. He looked like he'd escaped from a black-and-white movie.

Max's mouth dropped open.

"Go on, Max," said Harry. "Keep Larry

company while I go grocery shopping. Today is Customer Appreciation Day. Free Ding Dongs!"

"I don't think so," said Max.

"Aw, go on," said Harry. "Larry's a hoot. You'll see."

"I'll race ya!" shouted Larry, shooting out the door.

By the time Max got to the yard, Larry had disappeared.

"He's fast," Max said to no one.

CHAPTER 3

I STOPPED FOR PIZZA

When Max got to the coach house, Larry was sitting on the steps. "What took you so long?" he asked.

"I stopped for pizza," said Max.

"You're funny. I'm gonna like having you around." Larry got up and slid open the window. "In you go."

"What's wrong with the door?"

"It's locked. Dog swallowed the key."

"Grandpa doesn't have a dog."

"Tell that to the crazy mutt that keeps

coming around," said Larry.

Max climbed through the window. Larry walked through the wall.

The office was covered with cobwebs. It was obvious no one had been in it for years — that is, no one except Larry. Max spotted a metal filing cabinet, a bookcase, a typewriter, an old oak desk and a wooden coatrack with a brown coat on it.

"Cool coat," said Max.

"Try it on!" said Larry.

Max lifted the coat and shook it, sending up a cloud of dust. Then he slipped it on. It almost reached the floor.

Larry grinned. "A perfect fit!"

Max loved it. The sleeves were a bit long, but other than that, he wouldn't have changed a thing.

"Harry bought me that coat when I was a skinny kid and had just graduated from detective school," said Larry.

"It's not a typical detective's coat," said Max.

"Harry's not typical."

Max walked across the room, taking in some of the more unusual sights — a picture of a rooster, a snowman wearing a Hawaiian shirt … a cowboy hat. When he got to the desk, he slid into the swivel chair and spun around.

"I used to spin around every day," said Larry, "until the time I barfed up green candy floss."

"Candy floss?" said Max.

"The circus was in town."

As Max started to get up, Larry said, "Open the top drawer. Open it. Open it."

Max pulled open the drawer. Inside were lots of loose papers and a detective's notebook. It had a pencil tucked into the coil.

"You can have that if you like," said Larry.

Max smiled. "Thanks." He slipped the notebook into his pocket.

"Now try bottom left."

Max pulled open the bottom drawer on the left side of the desk. It was full of old comic books called *Starchy*.

"They're my *favorite*," gushed Larry. "You gotta read them. Starchy's this kid who turns into a *superhero* at eight o'clock every night. He can't fly — but he can run fast."

NINCOMPOOP?

Just as Max was lifting out the comic books, Larry burst out crying. "I can't *stand* myself," he sobbed, flinging himself on top of the desk. Max leaped out of the chair. "I've *ruined* the Monroe name. It used to stand for something. Now, because of me, it stands for ... for ... *nin-com-poooop!*"

"Nincompoop?"

"I deserve to be tarred and feathered!" wailed Larry.

"You're being too hard on yourself."

"I deserve to be beaten with a rubber hose!"

"Uncle Larry, calm down."

"I deserve to be dropped from a tree … on my *head*!"

Max tried not to laugh.

"If *ooooonly* I could have a second chance. That's all I want — a second chance to make things *riiiight*."

At that very moment … the phone rang.

CHAPTER 4

PRETTY PLEASE, WITH A CHERRY ON TOP?

Larry jumped off the desk and stared at the phone. "That phone hasn't rung in twenty years! Who could be calling?"

"Why don't you answer it and find out?" asked Max.

"Oh, no! I couldn't!"

Larry paced back and forth, wringing his hands. Then he spun around. "You answer it, Max!"

"Who, me?"

"*Pleeease?*"

Max shook his head. "I don't think so, Uncle Larry."

"Pretty please, with a cherry on top?"

Larry sounded so desperate that Max gave in and picked up the receiver. "Hello?"

"Larry, is that you?" asked the voice on the other end of the line.

"No … it's Max."

"This is Marty Macbee. Can I talk to Larry? It's an emergency!"

Max covered the mouthpiece. "It's Marty Macbee. He wants to talk to you."

"Why would he want to talk to me? I'm dead!"

"Want me to tell him?"

"Yeah, yeah. Go ahead."

Max cleared his throat. "I'm sorry, but —"

Suddenly, Larry started waving his arms, motioning for him to stop. Then he grabbed the phone, squeezed his eyes shut and said, "Hello?"

"Larry … this is Marty … Ted Crane's son. My father was a good friend of your mother's?"

Larry's eyes popped open. "Marty the *magician*? How ya doin'? I remember when you cut Aunt Gracie in half. Boy, did that turn out wrong."

"I'm in big trouble, Larry. You're the only detective I know. I *really* need your help."

"Hold on a minute, Marty. Gotta let the dog out." Larry threw the receiver into the drawer and slammed it shut.

CAN'T YOU SEE I'M DEAD?

"It's a case, Max! What should I do?"

"Take it!"

"Are you *nuts*? Can't you see I'm *dead*?"

Larry was jiggling up and down nervously and staring at the drawer.

Max said, "You're being given a second chance — just like you wished for."

Larry stopped jiggling. "You're right! This is a second chance! And maybe, if I *solve* this case …" His eyes got misty, and he sat down slowly. "The Monroe name will get its honor back."

He reached for the drawer again and then stopped. "Who am I kidding? I've *never* solved a case in my whole life! I'll screw this one up, just like all the others.

I can't do that to poor old Marty. I can't!"

He started bawling again.

"I'll help you," Max said.

Larry looked at Max with hope in his eyes. "Harry told me you love mysteries. But ... are you any good?"

"Yes."

CHAPTER 5

A MOTORCYCLE WITH A SIDECAR

Larry and Max walked quickly through the tall grass. "Marty's in town, at 15 Carson Lane," said Larry. "It's about fifteen minutes from here."

"How do we get there?" asked Max.

"You don't drive?"

"I'm *ten*."

"I drove when I was eight."

Max rolled his eyes. "Grandpa took the car to go shopping, and we can't wait for him to get back."

Larry thought for a second. "I've got it!"
He disappeared.

A few moments later, Max heard an engine roar. Looking around, he saw his uncle emerge from the garage sitting on a motorcycle with a sidecar. He wore an aviator's cap, goggles and a long coat over his body. He looked human.

Larry handed Max a hockey helmet. "Hop in!"

Max slipped on the helmet and jumped into the sidecar.

"Hold on, Max!" Larry gunned the motor and then shot out of the driveway like a cat on fire.

The motorcycle tore through the streets in town. In no time, they were screeching around the bend onto Carson Lane and whipping into the driveway of number 15. Larry slammed on the brakes so hard Max practically flew out of his seat.

The wooden house was two stories high with dark green shutters on every window. Pink and white balloons danced along the backyard fence. Between the balloons was a sign:

HAPPY BIRTHDAY DAISY!

ME? SCARE PEOPLE? NAH.
Larry slipped out of his coat, hat and goggles, and then headed toward the gate.

Max caught up to him. "You have to disappear now, Uncle Larry."

"Why?"

"Because you'll scare people, that's why."

"Me? Scare people? Nah."

"*Nah?*"

"I won't scare anybody, Max. Nobody can see me."

Larry walked through the fence.

"Uncle Larry!"

Larry came back.

"This may come as a news flash, but *I* can see you."

"Of course you can. I lowered my vibratory level to match your frequency so you can see me."

Max looked puzzled.

"Okay, okay. Think of it like this. Every radio station has its own signal, right? Well, I've tuned in to your signal. See?"

"If you tuned in to my signal, how did Marty talk to you?"

"Telephones convert sounds into electronic signals and then transmit them. I'm all energy. I can manipulate anything electrical. No problem."

Larry grinned and disappeared through the fence again.

CHAPTER 6

I THINK I'M GONNA FAINT

Max pushed open the gate and met Larry
on the other side. They looked around.
Spotting Marty was easy. He was wearing
a magician's hat and a long black satin
cape. Max walked over to him. "I'm Max
Monroe," he said. "Larry's nephew."

Marty looked behind Max, panic in his
eyes. "Where's Larry? I need Larry!"

"He couldn't make it. Sorry."

"Couldn't *make* it!?" wailed Marty. "What
do you *mean* he couldn't make it? I *need*

him! I need him *now*! I've got to find Daisy Dee in the next half hour or they'll throw me in *jail*!"

Larry's eyebrows shot up. "Ask Marty what he did."

"What did you do?" asked Max.

"I didn't *do* anything. But Daisy Dee has disappeared, and they're definitely gonna hold *me* responsible!" Marty's face turned a sickly shade of gray. "I think I'm gonna faint."

"Just tell him to fall this way, and I'll catch him," said Larry, holding out his arms.

"*No*," said Max.

"No, what?" asked Marty, looking confused.

"No … nothing," stammered Max.

Larry tapped Max on the shoulder. "Ask Marty how he gets those rabbits to sit still when they're in his hat."

"*Later,*" whispered Max.

"Later *what?*" asked Marty.

"Um … faint … you can faint later," said Max. "First, you have to find Daisy."

"Yes, yes, I have to find Daisy. What am I going to do? There's no time to call another detective, and Daisy's mother will be back soon. When she finds out little Daisy's disappeared, she'll *kill* me. Then she'll have me arrested!"

Larry frowned. "How can they arrest him if he's *dead?*"

Max shot his uncle a "stop interrupting" look, then turned back to Marty.

OH, GOSH

"Maybe I can help," said Max.

"*You?* Help *me?* You're just a kid, for crying out loud!"

"This is a kid's party. I'll fit right in."

"Good point," said Larry.

Marty didn't look convinced. "Oh, gosh, oh, gosh," he whimpered.

"What have you got to lose?" asked Max.

Marty nodded his head. "I guess you're right. Oh, gosh."

Thinking like a real detective, Max said, "Start at the beginning. And tell me everything that happened."

CHAPTER 7

THE CASE BEGINS

Marty took a deep breath. "My magic act was going just great. Everybody loved it. Then came the best part — where I make someone disappear from the Magic Box. I asked for a volunteer. All the kids wanted to be picked, but since it was Daisy's birthday, I chose her."

"How old is Daisy?" asked Max.

"Five."

"Then what did you do?"

"I opened the curtain at the front of the

box. Daisy stepped inside. I told her to stay very, very quiet. After I closed the curtain, I pushed a secret button at the side of the box. That made a panel slide across right in front of her. I waved my wand and said, 'Abracadabra!' When I pulled open the curtain, Daisy had disappeared. Everybody clapped and cheered. They didn't know she was *behind* the panel. Right?"

"Right!" said Larry, getting excited. "Then what happened?"

Max tried to ignore him. "*Then* what happened?" he asked.

GONE! KAPUT! VANISHED … !

"I closed the curtain and said more magic words. As I waved my wand, I pressed the secret button again. That made the panel slide back. When I flung open the curtain, Daisy was —"

Larry couldn't control himself. "Gone! Kaput! Vanished into thin air!"

"*Shh!*" hissed Max.

Marty looked hurt. "But you *asked* me to tell you what happened."

"I … I didn't mean you."

"What do you mean, you didn't mean me?" Marty looked around. "Nobody else is *here*."

"I'm here," said Max.

"Yeah? So?"

"So? … What did you do after Daisy disappeared?" Max tried to sound natural, but Marty was looking at him as though he was a nutcase. "Well?" said Max.

SMART MOVE

"Well … I had to think fast," said Marty. "I pretended Daisy disappearing was part of the show. I told the children there was a prize for whoever found her."

"Smart move," Max and Larry said at the same time.

"I thought so, too. But so far, *nobody's* found her."

"Was there any other way out of the Magic Box?" asked Max.

"There's an emergency door at the back. But it only opens from the outside. And I'm *sure* it was closed."

"Somebody must have opened the door and taken her out," said Max.

"Yes, but *who* took her?" asked Larry.

"Yes, but *where* is she?" sobbed Marty. "Please, you've got to find Daisy."

"I will," said Max.

Something about the way Max said "I will" made Marty feel better.

CHAPTER 8

LARRY REALLY WAS A BUMBLING DETECTIVE

Max looked around the yard. "Where's Daisy's mother?" he asked Marty.

"A man from the bakery dropped off Daisy's birthday cake. It had *Happy Birthday Lily* written on it by mistake. By the time Mrs. Dee noticed it, the driver was gone, so she jumped in the car and drove back to get the name changed."

"Good. That gives us more time."

"More time for what?" asked Larry.

Max looked at his uncle and shook his head. The newspapers had been right. Larry really was a bumbling detective.

"More time to find Daisy," whispered Max.

"Right!" said Larry.

STINK EYE

Max looked around and spotted a girl sitting alone on a bench.

"Who's she?" Max asked.

"That's Daisy's sister, Iris," answered Marty. "I don't think she likes me. Ever since I got here, she's been giving me the stink eye."

Larry laughed. "Better than pink eye."

"I'll start by talking to her," said Max.

As Max and Larry headed over to Iris, Larry started to get worried. "Maybe we're getting in over our heads, Max. A kid's disappeared. Shouldn't we call the police?"

"She didn't *really* disappear, Uncle Larry."

"Maybe she's been kidnapped! Did you think of that? *Huh?*"

"How would a kidnapper know the exact

time Daisy would be inside the Magic Box — or that Marty would even pick her? This is definitely an inside job."

"An inside job. Of course!"

As they got close to Iris, Larry whispered, "Be friendly, Max. People always tell you more when they think you're friendly."

Max put on a smile. "Hi. My name's Max."

"Don't tell me Mom hired *another* act. What do *you* do? Sing? Dance? Do the Hokey Pokey?"

"I did the Hokey Pokey once," said Larry. "But I sprained my back."

Max frowned at his uncle. "*Shhh.*"

Iris glared at Max. "Who are you *shushing?*"

"*Shoe.* I've got something in my shoe."

"Ask me if I care."

"Watch out," said Larry. "She might bite."

I'M GREAT. I'M FANTASTIC!

"You don't sound very happy," Max said to Iris. "Is something wrong?"

"*Wrong?* I'll tell you what's wrong! I practiced my magic act for two whole months to perform at Daisy's birthday. *Two whole months!* Then Mom said I wasn't quite ready and she went and hired Marty the Magnificent. Not quite ready? I'm great. I'm fantastic! My act was a whole lot better than stinky old Marty's."

"You must be pretty mad at Marty," said Max.

"You *bet* I am."

YOU'RE A MEANIE

"Daisy! Daisy!" called out a little girl. "Where are you?"

"Go look in the poison ivy," snapped Iris.

"Can you help me look?"

"No. Now beat it. I'm busy."

The little girl's mouth quivered and she ran off.

Larry leaned right into Iris's face and said, "You're a *meanie*." Then he vanished.

Max didn't like the way Iris acted either, but he needed information, and maybe she could help.

"I haven't met Daisy yet. Could you tell me a little bit about her?"

Iris rolled her eyes. "She loves piggyback rides and the color pink. Her favorite game is hide-and-seek. Her favorite food is

Marshmallow Mumbo. I'm bored now, so get lost."

"Just one more question? What was Daisy wearing when she disappeared?"

"Why do you want to know that?"

"Maybe I can find her and win the prize."

"Fine. She was wearing a pink dress and a sparkly tiara with fake diamonds on it."

"Did you see her disappear?"

"That's two questions. But just for the record, I was inside the house getting the Marshmallow Mumbo. It has to stay in the fridge till the last minute, or the heat from the sun will turn it to mush. Nobody likes mushy mumbo."

Talking about food made Max feel hungry. He said goodbye to Iris and headed over to the food table. On the way, he took his detective notebook out of his pocket and wrote …

Suspect #1 — Iris

Motive — Mad at Marty for taking her job

Iris wanted to do the magic show for Daisy's party. Her mother wouldn't let her, and hired Marty the Magnificent instead. By hiding Daisy, Iris would get Marty in big trouble and maybe even fired.

CHAPTER 9

HIDE-AND-SEEK

A spitball hit Max on the back of the neck. He swung around and spotted Larry waving a straw from a second-floor window. Larry was motioning for Max to come up.

Max went over to the back patio and in through the sliding doors. Once inside, he found the stairs and headed up to the second floor. Larry was at the end of the hallway.

"I have some information," whispered Larry.

"What is it?"

"I overheard a little girl say that Daisy's favorite game is hide-and-seek."

"Iris told me that, too."

"Did Iris *also* tell you that the last time Daisy had a sleepover, they played hide-and-seek? And did she tell you that Daisy hid in the *clothes* hamper? And did she tell you it was such a great hiding place that *nobody* found her?"

"Good work, Uncle Larry."

"Come in here. But don't make a sound."

Max followed Larry into a bedroom filled with kids' toys. A large picture of Daisy sat on the dresser.

Larry pointed to a pink clothes hamper with a flower design on the front. It was definitely big enough for a five-year-old to hide in.

Max and Larry tiptoed over to it. Just as Max was about to lift the lid, a sound came from behind them.

SHE'S GOTTA BE SOMEWHERE

"She's under the bed!" whispered Larry.

"Daisy?" said Max in a kind voice. "Are you hiding under the bed?"

He crouched down and lifted the blanket. A cute kid with no front teeth smiled at him. "She's not under here," the kid said, rolling out.

Max helped him up. "Keep trying. She's gotta be somewhere."

"Okay!" The kid dashed out of the room.

Max turned back to the hamper. He lifted the lid and stuck his arm down into the clothes. His hand reached the bottom.

"Nothing."

"Nothing?" Larry's voice cracked and his eyes got misty. He pulled out a hanky.

"What's wrong, Uncle Larry?"

"I was sure I'd solved the case!"

"Don't feel bad. It's a good piece of information."

Larry wiped his eyes. "Other rooms, other hampers?"

"Exactly."

Max and Larry made their way to the next bedroom. It had posters of a boy band on the wall, but there was no hamper.

"Try the closet," suggested Max.

Larry swung open the closet door. There was a giant pile of clothes on the floor.

Suddenly … the clothes moved.

CHAPTER 10

STRANGE THING TO HAVE UNDER A PILLOW

"She's here!" shouted Larry.

He jammed his hand into the pile of clothes and yanked out an arm. "Bingo!"

The arm belonged to the kid with no front teeth. When he saw his arm up in the air with nobody holding it, he screamed like crazy and ran out of the room.

"Darn," grumbled Larry. "Still no Daisy."

Max looked worried. "Uncle Larry, what if he tells someone what he saw?"

Larry slumped down on the bed and said, "Nobody would believe him."

Suddenly he jumped up and lifted the pillow, revealing a black cardboard tube. Max reached for the tube.

"Strange thing to have under a pillow, don't you think?" said Max.

"I kept a love letter from Diane Krolly under mine," said Larry. "Then my cousin Marvin found it and spread the juicy details all over school. I didn't speak to him for a month. Would have held out longer, but he gave me his peanut brittle." Larry sighed. "I never could resist peanut brittle …"

GOTCHA!

Max twisted the top of the tube, and out sprang a *huge* black snake.

"*AAAHHHHHHHH!*" Larry leaped onto the bed. "*AAHH! AAHH! AAHH!*"

"It's fake!" Max shouted over Larry's shrieks.

"*FAKE?!*" Larry shrieked back. "Are you *sure?*"

Max nodded. "Since when are ghosts afraid of snakes?"

"How would I know? They scared me when I was alive. I guess it stuck with me. But more to the point," he said, stepping down from the bed, "what kind of *lunatic* would play such a horrible trick?"

Max pulled a piece of paper out of the tube.

"What does it say?" asked Larry. "Show me. Show me."

Max held up the note for his uncle to see:

Gotcha!
Love, Nick.

"Who the heck is Nick?"

A car door slammed.

Larry went into panic mode. "Oh, no! Mrs. Dee's back!"

They raced over to the window and looked out. A little boy holding a present was coming up the walk, waving to someone in a dark blue car.

"It's not Mrs. Dee," said Max. "But she'll be back any minute, and we're no closer to solving the mystery."

CHAPTER 11

WHAT THE HECK IS
MARSHMALLOW MUMBO?

When they got back outside, Max and Larry heard kids laughing. Marty was pulling colored scarves out of his nose.

"Maybe Marty can give us another lead," said Max.

As they headed toward him, they passed the food table. Larry stopped. "Boy, this food sure looks *good.*"

"Too bad you can't eat," said Max.

"I can eat."

"You're a *ghost*. Where would the food go?"

Larry shrugged. "Beats me." He reached for some nachos.

Max watched as the nachos disappeared into Larry's mouth.

"Yummy," said Larry. "Try some."

"I feel like Marshmallow Mumbo," said Max.

Larry's eyebrows went up. "What the heck is Marshmallow Mumbo?"

"It's a dessert made with pudding and marshmallows. Iris said she brought some out when Marty was doing the Magic Box trick."

Larry and Max looked all over the table.

"Nothing here is made out of marshmallows," said Larry, reaching for some strawberries.

Max turned and headed back toward the house.

"Where are you going?" asked Larry.

"I want to check something. I'll be right back."

Max opened the patio doors and made his way through the family room and into the kitchen. Two kids were checking the cabinet under the sink. "Daisy's not here," he heard one of them say.

"Let's try the closet!" said the other one. They raced out.

Left alone in the kitchen, Max opened the refrigerator door. There was nothing that looked like Marshmallow Mumbo in there either. When he got back outside, he told Larry about the missing mumbo. "Somebody's obviously taken it."

"Or eaten it!" said Larry.

"If somebody ate it, there should be an empty dish somewhere."

Suddenly, water splashed them. A boy with jet-black hair sticking up from his head was shaking himself dry. He had just stepped out of the swimming pool.

CHICK-CHICK-CHICKEN

"Hi. My name's Nick. I'm the chef today."

"That's snake-in-the-can Nick!" said Larry.

"What'll you have?" continued Nick. "Hamburgers, pizza or chick-chick-chicken?"

"Chicken sounds great," said Max.

Nick pulled a rubber chicken out of his swimming trunks. "*HA! HA! HA!*"

"Neat trick," said Larry. "Ask him what else he's got in there."

"Looks like there's more than one magician here today," said Max.

"I'm not a magician," sniffed Nick. "I'm a practical joker. I play *tricks* on people. I once switched baby carriages at the park and Mom came home with *twins*. The newspaper even wrote a story about me."

Nick ran off laughing. As he turned the corner, his wet feet slid on the grass and he fell on his butt.

Larry burst out laughing. "Now, *that's* funny."

Max pulled out his notebook and wrote …

Suspect #2 — Nick

Motive — Practical joke

"If Nick took Daisy," said Max, "it would be his greatest practical joke. People would talk about it at birthday parties for years to come. He'd be known as the kid who outsmarted the magician, and he'd be famous."

"Right!" said Larry.

CHAPTER 12

SURPRISE ME

POP!

Larry dove to the ground. Max spun around and spotted a clown blowing up balloons.

"Relax, Uncle Larry. It was just a balloon."

"I knew that. I thought I saw a dime down here."

Max made his way over to the clown. "You make cool balloon animals."

The clown beamed. "Thank you very much!" He shook Max's hand. "I'm

Skippy the Clown. Would you like a balloon animal? Maybe a giraffe — or a pony?"

"I'm trying to find Daisy," Max said. "Did you happen to see her?"

"No!" Skippy snapped. Then, quickly changing his tone, he asked, "What kind of animal can I make for you?"

"Surprise me."

MAGIC TRICKS. BIG DEAL.

Skippy blew up some long, skinny balloons. He twisted them this way and that. A second later, he was holding a dinosaur.

"That's awesome," said Max.

"Will you spread the word around?" Skippy asked sadly. "Business has been kind of slow. No matter how hard I try — making balloon animals, riding my minibike or telling jokes — I get nowhere. All kids want to see is Marty the Magnificent. Magic tricks. *Big* deal."

"That was some trick, making Daisy disappear. You sure you haven't seen her?"

"I told you I haven't seen her! But there's one good thing that would come out of it if she really has disappeared. It'll be the end of Marty the Magnificent!"

Skippy threw the dinosaur on the ground and stomped away.

Larry picked it up. "Touchy guy."

Max noticed some kids staring at the balloon hovering in midair. He grabbed it fast.

"Skippy is jealous of Marty's popularity," explained Max. He opened his notebook and wrote …

Suspect #3 — Skippy the Clown

Motive — Jealousy

"If Skippy hid Daisy, everybody would blame Marty. Soon, parents would hear about it. Marty wouldn't get hired for other parties, and business would pick up for Skippy again."

"Right!" said Larry.

Max tucked the notebook into his pocket and looked at his uncle. "I'm ready to take a look at the scene of the crime."

CHAPTER 13

NEAT TRICK, EH?

Max and Larry made their way to the far side of the house. The Magic Box, covered with stars, stood right in the center of a row of high bushes.

"Those bushes would hide anyone walking behind the Magic Box," said Max.

They moved closer. Larry whipped open the velvet curtain and stepped inside. Then he pulled the curtain closed.

"Push the button, Max," he called out.

Max looked along the sides of the Magic

Box and found a small button on the left side. When he pushed it, a wooden panel slid right in front of Larry. When Max opened the curtain, the box looked empty.

Larry stuck his head through the panel and grinned. "Neat trick, eh?"

Max pushed the button again and the panel slid back into its hiding place. Larry stepped through the back of the Magic Box. A second later, he swung open the back door. "Someone definitely opened this door to let Daisy out," he said.

HURRY! HURRY! PLEASE!

"There you are, Max."

Max turned to see Marty. His face was lined with worry. "Have you found Daisy?"

"Not yet, but I'm working on it."

"Mrs. Dee will be back any minute! Hurry! Hurry! Please!"

Some kids grabbed Marty's hands and dragged him off. Max made his way around the bushes to the back of the Magic Box.

"Hey, Max!" shouted Larry. "Look there!" He pointed to the ground near the Magic Box. "A wiener dog balloon! *Skippy* took Daisy!"

"Maybe," said Max. "But let's check for other clues."

As they looked around, a flash of light caught Max's eye. "What's that?"

"What's what?" asked Larry.

"There it is again. Something in the bushes is reflecting the sun."

Max walked over to the third bush from the Magic Box and parted the branches. Resting on one of them was a small, sparkly tiara. He held it up. "Iris told me Daisy was wearing a tiara. It must have fallen off when she passed by this bush."

"The plot thickens," said Larry, wiggling his eyebrows.

NOBODY COULD GAIN WEIGHT THAT FAST

Max rested the tiara back on the branch and went looking for more clues.

"Footprints, Uncle Larry."

"Where?"

"Right here." He pointed to the ground behind the Magic Box. "They go in that direction." Max pointed toward the side of the house.

Max bent down to examine the footprints more closely.

"Look at this, Uncle Larry."

Larry bent down next to him.

"The footprints start off light, but the prints leading away from the Magic Box sink deeper into the ground."

Larry scratched his head. "Nobody could gain weight *that* fast."

Max stood up and looked at his uncle. "Oh, yes, they could."

CHAPTER 14

MAX SOLVES THE CASE

Marty asked the three suspects — Iris, Nick and Skippy — to meet at the Magic Box. When they had all gathered, Max said, "I've looked carefully at all the clues, and I know who took Daisy Dee."

Iris, Nick and Skippy eyeballed each other.

"Marty mentioned that there's a back door on the Magic Box that can only be opened from the *outside*. Someone opened the door and took Daisy. When they did, they left footprints in the dirt."

Max moved closer to the footprints. "The footprints start from where the grass ends and go straight to the Magic Box. Then the same footprints continue *away* from the box."

Everyone's eyes followed the line of footprints.

YOU ARE A SMART COOKIE, AREN'T YOU?

"Iris told me Daisy was wearing a tiara," said Max. "There it is in the bushes. So she probably went that way."

"If Daisy went that way," said Marty, "why aren't *her* footprints on the ground, too?"

"Yeah, Sherlock," said Nick, smirking. "Answer *that* one."

"It's a good question. Whoever took Daisy must have *lifted* her out of the Magic Box," said Max, "then carried her. The extra weight made the footprints leading away from the Magic Box sink deeper into the dirt."

Larry looked impressed. "You *are* a smart cookie, aren't you?"

Max smiled at his uncle. Then he turned his attention to Skippy. "Skippy, one of your balloon animals is on the ground beside the Magic Box."

Larry's eyes lit up. "I told you it was Skippy!"

Skippy shook his head vigorously. "That doesn't prove anything."

"You're right," said Max. "It doesn't."

Larry frowned. "It doesn't?"

"You made lots of balloons, and any of the kids could have dropped it." Skippy breathed a sigh of relief. "But there's still the matter of footprints."

Skippy pointed to his shoes. "Do *these* shoes look like they made *those* footprints? My clown shoes are *huge*. They would have left a much bigger print!"

"Do you wear regular shoes under your clown shoes?" asked Max.

Skippy gulped. "Yes. But they're glued in! I swear!"

He whipped off one of his clown shoes and tugged on the inner shoe, showing everyone that it was glued in tightly. "My clown shoes kept falling off, so I glued my shoes into them."

WHAT KIND OF DORK WEARS SHOES WITH A BATHING SUIT?

Max turned to Nick. "Where are your shoes, Nick?"

"What kind of dork wears shoes with a bathing suit?"

"Do you want me to answer him?" asked Larry.

Max frowned at his uncle then turned back to Nick. "I was just checking. Maybe you wore them before changing into your bathing suit."

"Well, I *didn't*. I live next door and came over in my swimsuit. If you don't believe me, go ask my mom."

"I believe you," said Max. "But the footprints were definitely made by shoes."

He slowly turned to face Iris. "So, that leaves you."

WHAT DID YOU DO WITH THE MARSHMALLOW MUMBO?

"*Me?*" Iris put on her snooty voice. "You've *got* to be kidding."

"You said you were inside the house when Daisy disappeared," said Max.

"I *was* inside, getting the Marshmallow Mumbo."

"Then why is nothing on the food table made of marshmallows?"

"Yeah," said Larry. "What did you do with the Marshmallow Mumbo?"

Max continued. "During Marty's disappearing act, you went into the house to get the Marshmallow Mumbo, like you said, but you didn't put it on the food table. Instead, you came out the back door and snuck up to the Magic Box from behind. *You're* the one who lifted Daisy out. You're the one who carried her away — probably on your back so that you could carry the Marshmallow Mumbo at the same time. Daisy didn't make a fuss because she trusted you. And what kid doesn't like a piggyback ride?"

Iris rolled her eyes. "And just what *motive* would I have for taking Daisy?"

"With Daisy missing," explained Max, "your mom would blame Marty. You wanted to get back at him for taking your job — the magic act that you worked so hard on."

Iris exclaimed, "*Two whole months* I

spent practicing that magic act! *Two whole months!*"

Just then, Daisy's mother pulled into the driveway.

Iris crossed her arms. "Even if I *did* take Daisy, you'll never find her."

"You gotta tell us where you hid her," begged Marty.

"Nope."

"Iris, *please.*"

Iris stuck her fingers in her ears. "Lah-dee-dah. Lah-dee-dah. I can't hear you."

"Oh, gosh. Oh, gosh." Once again, Marty looked like he was going to faint.

Larry got an idea. He leaned over and whispered something to Max. Max's face lit up and he whispered something to Marty.

OLLY OLLY OXEN FREE!

In a loud voice, Marty called out, "Olly olly oxen free!" That's the signal for everybody playing hide-and-seek to come out of their hiding places.

A second later, Daisy stuck her head out the attic window.

"Here I am! I win! I win! Nobody found me!"

Daisy's smiling face was covered with … Marshmallow Mumbo!

BRILLIANT! ABSOLUTELY BRILLIANT!

Max couldn't wait to tell his grandfather about his adventure. He and Larry hopped onto the motorcycle and roared home.

Harry was on the couch, knitting, when they arrived. "Where have you two been?" he asked.

"Solving our first mystery!" boasted Larry. "I was brilliant! Absolutely brilliant!"

Max looked at him.

"Oh, yeah, and Max was brilliant, too."

"Well done, boys! I'm proud of you both! How about we celebrate with ice cream and apple pie?"

Larry rubbed his hands together. "Sounds yummy."

As they ate their ice cream and pie,
Max asked, "What are you knitting,
Grandpa?"

"A hat for the dog!"

Max's eyebrows went up.

SPOT THE DIFFERENCE

Detectives have to be observant.
Can you find five differences between these
two pictures?

1. One of Max's coat buttons is missing.
2. The cobweb is missing beside the rooster picture.
3. One of the falling sheets of paper is missing.
4. One of Larry's suspenders is missing.
5. The snowman is facing the other way.

DON'T MISS CASE #2 ...

the GHOST *and* MAX MONROE

CASE #2
THE MISSING ZUCCHINI

"They want me to find their zucchini, Uncle Larry."
"So? Sherlock Holmes had lots of unusual cases."
Max shook his head. "I seriously doubt anyone ever asked
him to find a missing vegetable."

The giant vegetable competition at the Harrow Harvest
Fair is a day away, and the Zamboni sisters' 200-pound
zucchini has been stolen. Max and Uncle Larry take the
case — but looking for a missing vegetable? Max can't
help but think it will be dull as dirt ... until they start
digging deeper. Can Max and Uncle Larry uncover the
thief, and the giant zucchini, before the big day?

The Ghost and Max Monroe series continues with
another hilarious, fast-paced mystery, featuring a sharp
ten-year-old detective and his frightfully funny sidekick.

The Ghost and Max Monroe
Case #2: The Missing Zucchini

L. M. Falcone

HC 978-1-77138-154-3
$12.95 US • $12.95 CDN

PB 978-1-77138-018-8
$6.95 US • $6.95 CDN